Wolf's Mindful Tales

The Big Bad Wolf Learns to Chill Out

Illustrator El Corazón de Malena

www.LauraLinnKnight.com

LAURA
LINN KNIGHT
Parenting with magic

To Oliver and Grace: May you always keep wishing on dandelion flowers. Huff, puff, huff, puff. - **LLK**

Con todo mi amor para: Blanca, Jorge, David y Rosa, gracias por siempre creer en mi. - **S**

This book is for

_____

Wolf's Mindful Tales

The Big Bad Wolf Learns to Chill Out

Story by Laura Linn Knight
Art by El Corazón de Malena

Once upon a time...

there was a Big Bad Wolf who played awful tricks. He huffed and puffed down a house made of straw. He huffed and puffed down a house built with sticks. And he almost blew over a house stacked with bricks.

Over time, the Big Bad—and very lonely—Wolf became tired of always being the bad guy. After all, working as a villain is a very isolating business.

Wolf grew sad and wished he had a pack to play with.

Wolf decided to change his menacing ways.
"No more *huffing*, no more *puffing*, no more
blowing houses down . . .

I will do more good from now on!"

Wolf rescued Little Bear's chair from Goldilocks.
The seat that fit Bear just right!

Wolf ferried the
Gingerbread Boy
away from Fox before
Fox could take a bite.

Wolf saved a
cursed frog and
turned him into a
Prince. A Prince
ready for the ball!

Wolf made new friends with all of his good deeds,
but there was one problem he could not ignore.

Wolf missed his *huff* and *puff*.

He loved the air tickling his throat when
he breathed in a big *HUFF*.

His heart fluttered with happiness when
he pushed out a mighty *PUFF*.

At home, Wolf *huffed* and *puffed* in front of the mirror.

Huff, Puff, Huff, Puff

He *huffed* and *puffed* with a rubber ducky
in the bubbles.

Huff, Puff, Huff, Puff

He *huffed* and *puffed* himself to sleep at night.

Huff, Puff, Huff, Puff

"I wish I could *huff* and *puff* with my friends, but I have promised to do good."

Wolf tied on his cape and dashed out the door for another day of saving and protecting.

As Wolf hid Snow White from the Wicked Queen,
his ears perked up and his nose sniffed . . .

FIRE!

Wolf raced through Fairy Tale Land to the enchanted forest. Smoke twirled out of Little Pig's chimney.

"Help us!" Little Pig screamed. "You must *huff* and *puff* and blow the fire out!"

"I can't!" Wolf cried.

He buried his head in his paws. He didn't want his *huff* and *puff* to land him in trouble again!

Wolf made a plan.

As the flames danced, Wolf shouted instructions.

"Backs straight! Stand tall.

Deep HUFF in. Let your belly fill with air.

Big PUFF out.

Blow the air awwAAAYYY."

Together, the characters *huffed*, and
they *puffed*, *huffed* and *puffed*.

"Repeat!" Wolf said.

Huff, Puff, Huff, Puff

"Try again!"

HUFF, PUFF, HUFF, PUFF

They *huffed* and *puffed* until they were blue in
the face. Alas, they couldn't blow the flames out.

"Make my wish come true and
help us too," begged Little Pig.

"OK! That's what good wolves do," said Wolf.

He stepped in line with his friends.

The air tickled Wolf's throat as he
breathed in a big *HUFF.*

His heart fluttered with happiness as he
pushed out a mighty *PUFF.*

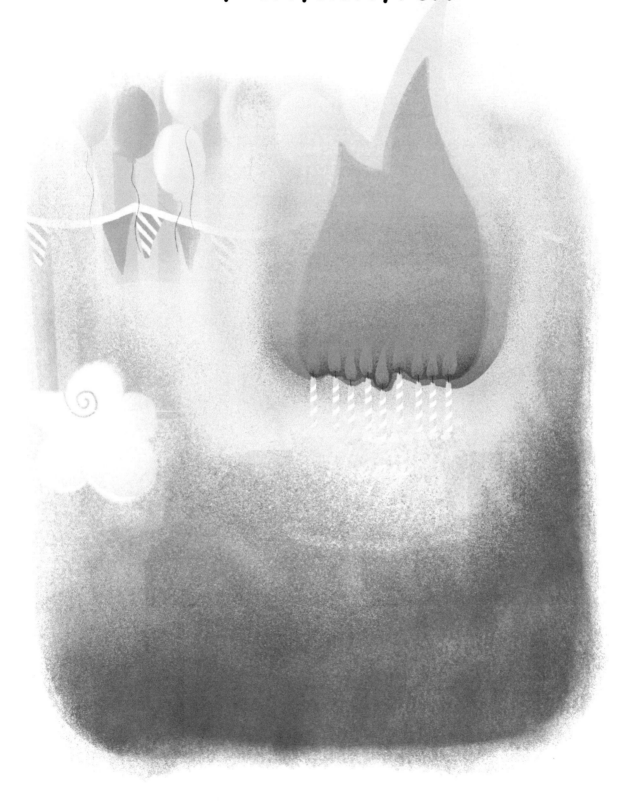

HUFF, PUFF, HUFF, PUFF
HUFF, PUFF, HUFF, PUFF
HUFF, PUFF, HUFF, PUFF
HUFF, PUFF, HUFF, PUFF

Together, they blew the fire out!

"Happy birthday, Little Pig!"

Wolf sang.

"You did it, Wolf. You saved the day.
Your *huffs* and *puffs* are here to stay!"

From then on, Wolf promised to use his *huffs* and *puffs* to spread calm all around while he saved and protected his town!

And they all ate cake and . . .
lived happily (and peacefully) ever after.

The End.
May all of your wishes come true!

How Huffs and Puffs Can Calm Your Body and Brighten Your Day

Wolf used his *huffs* and *puffs* to save Little Pig's party and spread calm all around his town. You can use your *huffs* and *puffs* to calm your body down too! Practice doing *huffs* and *puffs* three to six times in a row. This can be done anywhere—seated in the classroom, out in the schoolyard, at the park, or lying in bed.

When you are ready, imagine you are blowing out birthday candles on Little Pig's birthday cake, and chant this:

Back straight. Sit up tall!

Deep HUFF in. Let my belly fill with air.

Big PUFF out. Blow the air awwAAAYYY.

AND/OR

Back straight. Sit up tall!

Deep HUFF in for a count of 1, 2, 3.

Big PUFF out for a count of 1, 2, 3.

Have fun trying both breathing techniques, and see which one you like best.

Color Me Calm

Coloring is another awesome calm-down tool. When you color, your brain focuses on being creative, so it can take a break from your worries or frustrations. That helps your body and your mind chill out! You can download these coloring pages from **www.LauraLinnKnight.com/coloring**

I am Kind

Kids, did you know . . .

scientists have studied *huffing* and *puffing?* This type of deep breathing calms your body and makes you feel better. Think of your body as a car, racing around and burning lots of gas. *Huffing* and *puffing* slows and steadies your body like brakes in a car.

* A Note to Grown-ups:

An interactive way to have your child *huff* and *puff* with you is by holding out your fingers and pretending they are Little Pig's birthday cake candles. With each *huff* and *puff* from your child, lower one of your fingers. As you invite your child to *huff* and *puff* like Wolf, it will help them to regulate emotionally (and will teach your child how the breath is a wonderful self-regulation tool).

Hey, kids!
You're a huffing and puffing star! Want to learn more of Wolf's cool calm-down tools and follow all of his adventures in Fairy Tale Land? Ask your grown-up to help you find more awesome activities for you and your family at www.LauraLinnKnight.com.

Hey, parents!
Want to understand the why behind your child's emotional dysregulation and your power struggles? Looking for more parenting tools that help you create lasting positive change in your family and a more peaceful, joyful home? Check out Laura's book *Break Free from Reactive Parenting: Gentle-Parenting Tips, Self-Regulation Strategies, and Kid-Friendly Activities for Creating a Calm and Happy Home.*

Praise for Break Free from Reactive Parenting:

"Dear frustrated parents, this book is really good medicine. It has wisdom and humor and honesty that will help, calming your heart and inspiring your best parenting."
—Jack Kornfield, PhD, author of *A Path with Heart*

"At last, a parenting book with practical, pragmatic, and proactive strategies that we can actually use and that actually work! Thank you, Laura Linn Knight, for creating this beautiful guide that allows us to be the parents we always wanted to be."
—Christopher Willard, author of *Growing Up Mindful* and *Alphabreaths*

About the Author

Laura Linn Knight

@lauralinnknight

The Writer

Once upon a time, Laura Linn Knight spent her days teaching kindergarten and first grade. She loved helping her students learn and grow!

When Laura became a mom, she knew she wanted to find more ways to support kids and their grown-ups, so today she teaches families how to create calmer homes by giving them tools and ideas that can help them work together.

Laura has shared her work on television, on podcasts, and in radio interviews, and she is the author of several books, which makes her very proud. ***Wolf's Mindful Tales*** are her first books for kids, and she can't wait to write more!

Fun Facts about Laura:

When she's not teaching and writing, she loves spending time with her husband, her two kids, her two cats, and her two dogs.

She enjoys traveling all over the world. Her favorite places to visit are Colombia, Costa Rica, and camping in California.

A few of her favorite things to do are read, dance, and go on adventures with her family.

About the Illustrator

In a place far, far away on the other side of the ocean, in a beautiful country called Colombia, lives Sara López.

She loved art and painting from a very young age, so when she grew up, she became an illustrator. She changed her name to Malena and created her own world called the Heart of Malena. There she paints and illustrates everything she loves.

She learned to share her art, because the world will always be more beautiful in color.

Fun Facts about Malena:

Her favorite colors are yellow and pink.
Her zodiac sign is Pisces.
She loves the sea and the sun.
Her spirit animal is a bunny.
She always listens to music while she draws!

Psst ... Here's a creativity tip from Malena:

If your dream is to become an artist, draw every day. You will get better with practice. And listen to your favorite music while you draw—it will inspire you and fill you with happiness.

Sara López Mesa
@elcorazondemalena

The Illustrator

Made in the USA
Monee, IL
21 July 2024

62334051R00031